Scribbleville

by
Peter Holwitz

PHILOMEL BOOKS

NEW YORK

PHILOMEL BOOKS

A division of Penguin Young Readers Group

Published by The Penguin Group

Penguin Group (USA) Inc., 375 Hudson Street, New York, NY 10014, U.S.A.

Penguin Group (Canada), 10 Alcorn Avenue, Toronto, Ontario, Canada M4V 3B2 (a division of Pearson Penguin Canada Inc.)

Penguin Books Ltd, 80 Strand, London WC2R 0RL, England.

Penguin Ireland, 25 St. Stephen's Green, Dublin 2, Ireland (a division of Penguin Books Ltd.)

Penguin Books India Pvt Ltd, 11 Community Centre, Panchsheel Park, New Delhi - 110 017, India.

Penguin Group (NZ), Cnr Airborne and Rosedale Roads, Albany, Auckland, New Zealand (a division of Pearson New Zealand Ltd).

Penguin Books (South Africa) (Pty) Ltd, 24 Sturdee Avenue, Rosebank, Johannesburg 2196, South Africa.

Penguin Books Ltd, Registered Offices: 80 Strand, London WC2R 0RL, England.

Published simultaneously in Canada. Manufactured in China by South China Printing Co. Ltd.

Design by Gina DiMassi. Text set in Humana Sans Medium.

The art for this book was created with pencil, Magic Marker, and chalk on vellum.

Library of Congress Cataloging-in-Publication Data

Holwitz, Peter.

Scribbleville / by Peter Holwitz.   p. cm.

Summary: When a man who is straight as a stick arrives in Scribbleville,
he is met with resistance until one child shows everyone that there is beauty in every kind of line, straight or scribbled.

[1. Toleration–Fiction. 2. Change–Fiction. 3. Line (Art)–Fiction. 4. Stories in rhyme.] I. Title.

PZ8.3.H745Sc 2005   [E]–dc22   2004016575

ISBN 0-399-24303-8

1 3 5 7 9 10 8 6 4 2

First Impression

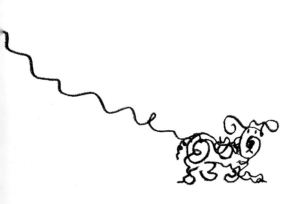

for Betsy

Just up the road, beyond that hill,
there's a little town called Scribbleville.

You'll know when you're there. It's easy to tell.
The signs on the street don't read so well.
And the folks you might meet—they all walk with wiggles.
Their knees are in knots and their feet are all squiggles.
They have scribbled houses. They wear scribbled hats.
They walk scribbled dogs and "chicken-scratch" cats.
You can search high and low. You can scour the town—
a single straight line will never be found.

Until the day a stranger came.
And Scribbleville was never the same.
He drove a straight big truck through the middle of town—
long thick lines with wheels big and round.
It was tough to tell—he passed so quick—
but the man in the truck looked straight as a stick.

He parked his truck and began to unload
near a scribbly tree on a scribbly road.
He built a house. It was perfectly straight,
with a tall pointed roof and a white picket gate.
Well, out on the street the word spread quick
of the straight new house, and the man like a stick.
"Have you seen him?" they asked. "He showed up today."
"Where does he come from? How long will he stay?"
"Why would a man so straight and so slim
want to live in a town where no one's like him?"

Wherever he went, the people would stare.
"Look at his clothes." "Who cuts his hair?"
"He doesn't fit in. He looks all wrong.
Someone should tell him he doesn't belong!"

The very next day, the stranger worked hard.
He planted a tree and put grass in his yard.
Then a woman walked up. Her hair was a mess.
She wore a big smile and a red scribbled dress.
"Good morning," she said as she played with her hair.
"That's a beautiful house—I can't help but stare."
"Thank you," he said, and gave her a smile.
They stood at his gate and chatted awhile.

They had lunch the next day. They had dinner too.
They did all the things that new friends do.
But the folks around town—in the stores, on the street—
they threw up their hands and stomped their feet.

Her friends all said,
"She's lost her mind."

"She's gone too far."
"She's crossed the line!"

"I admit," she said, as her
scribbled head shook,
"on the outside he's odd, but
that's not where I look."

She changed her hair. He said, "It looks great!"
The ends were scribbled but the sides were straight.
They took long walks. They shopped at the store.
He bought a new shirt he might not have before.

In Scribbleville Park there gathered a crowd.
They threw up their hands and shouted aloud.

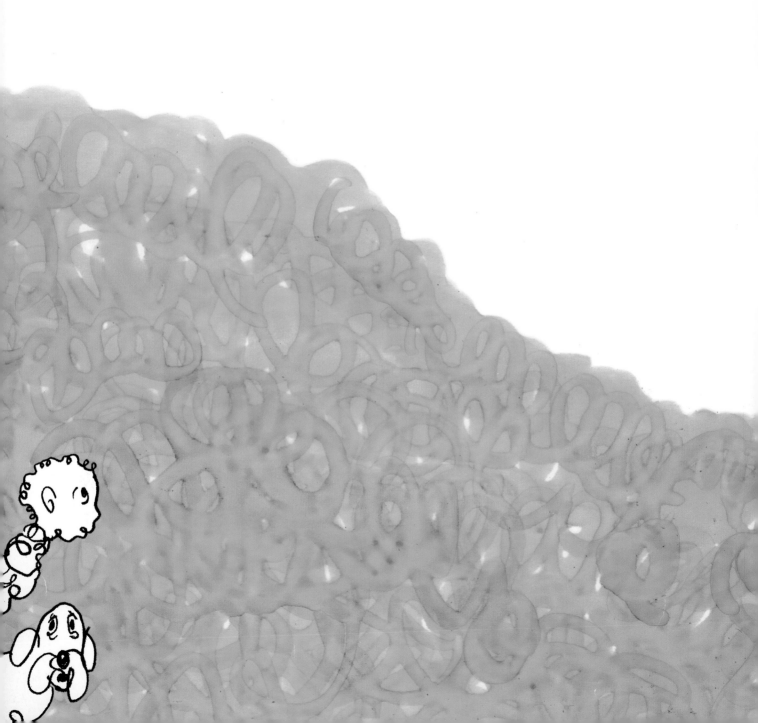

"It starts with one, but that's not where it ends.
He'll pick up the phone and call all his friends.
And they'll move here too. It will cause such a fuss.
There'll be more of *them* than there are of us!"

That night, a kid sat down at his table
and drew from his mind some things he was able.
A scribbled tree. A "chicken-scratch" cat.
He drew himself with a scribbled hat.
But then he drew something totally new.
A drawing that no one in town would do.

He drew a house and a picket gate.
Some of it scribbled,
and some of it straight.
Lines, thick and thin—
some short—some taller.
He drew big scribbles.
Some of them smaller.

His mother smiled. His dad scratched his head.

"That's a beautiful house," is what they said.

And his friends at school were all surprised.

His teacher stared with open eyes.

They all agreed his art was great.

Just enough scribble and just enough straight.

So his friends all did what kids will do.

They drew straight lines and scribbles too.

In every house, a few days later—
on every scribbled refrigerator—
every mom and dad there was
did what every parent does.

And then one day—you might guess why—
a teacher wore a straight new tie.
At first it seemed strange 'cause the change was so new.
But soon a few kids wore straight lines too.

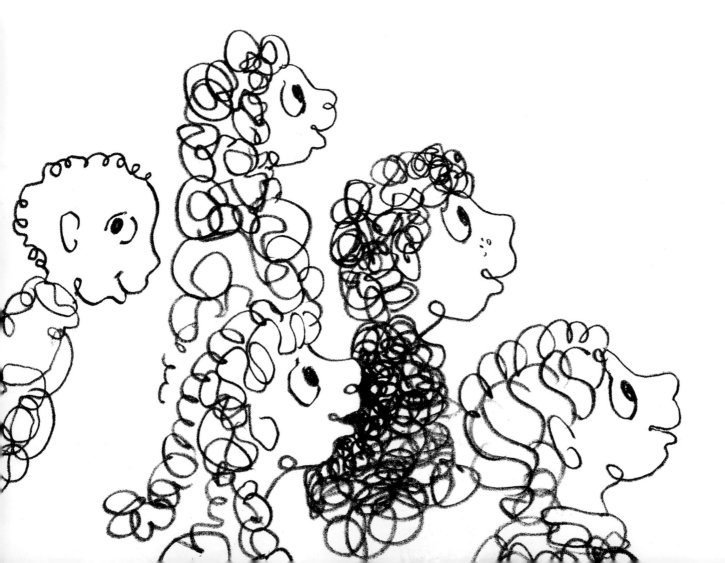

And before too long, no one was staring.
The lines looked good with what they were wearing.

It's tough to say—to pick one day.
Things never change overnight.
But before too long, what once felt wrong,
started to feel a bit right.
An old restaurant put up a straight new sign.
Business was good. There was always a line.

Time went by. Things changed a lot.
New folks moved in. Some scribbled—some not.
The town didn't look like it once did before.
And the stranger wasn't so strange anymore.

He married the woman in the red scribbled dress.
Her gown was gorgeous. Her hair was a mess.

They built a new house with a white picket gate.
The shrubs were scribbled but the grass was straight.
They had two kids. One was scribbled. One wasn't.
What does it matter? Maybe it doesn't!

Just up the road, beyond that hill,
there's a little town called Scribbleville.
And you'll know when you're there. It's easy to tell.
Whoever you are, you'll fit in well.